Glendale Library, Arts & Culture Dept.

3 9010 05715039 7

CHILDREN'S BOOK

NO LONGER PROPERTY OF
GLENDALE LIBRARY,
ARTS, AND CULTURE DEPT

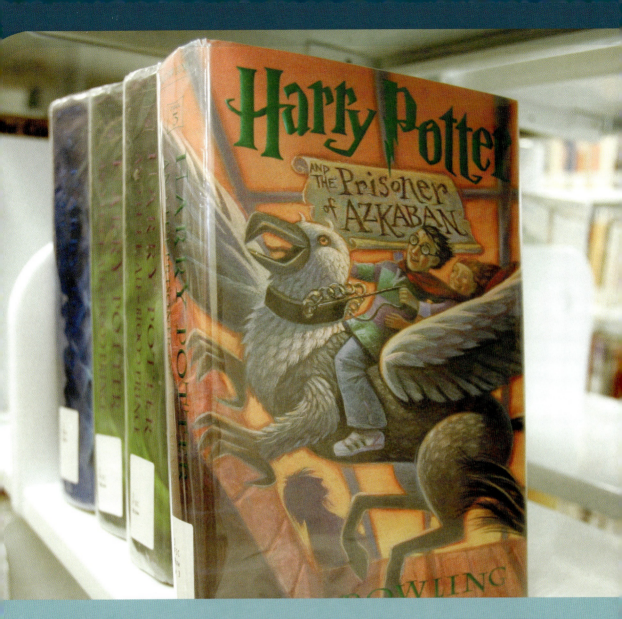

THE 12 MOST INFLUENTIAL
BOOKS OF ALL TIME

by Barbara Krasner

12 STORY LIBRARY

j 028.09 KRA

www.12StoryLibrary.com

Copyright © 2018 by 12-Story Library, Mankato, MN 56003. All rights reserved. No part of this book may be reproduced or utilized in any form or by any means without written permission from the publisher.

12-Story Library is an imprint of Bookstaves and Press Room Editions

Produced for 12-Story Library by Red Line Editorial

Photographs ©: Michael Conroy/AP Images, cover, 1; duncan1890/iStockphoto, 4; Alastair Muir/Rex Features/AP Images, 5; North Wind Picture Archives, 6; Bain News Service/Bain Collection/Library of Congress, 7; Everett Historical/Shutterstock Images, 9, 13, 17, 24; William R. Howell/Liljenquist Family Collection of Civil War Photographs/Library of Congress, 10; Courier Company/Theatrical Poster Collection/Library of Congress, 11; Patrick_Gijsbers/iStockphoto, 12; akg-images/Newscom, 14; Jeff Malet Photography/Newscom, 15; Fred Stein/picture-alliance/dpa/AP Images, 16, 28; AP Images, 18, 29; PongMoji/Shutterstock Images, 19; Rena Schild/Shutterstock Images, 20; Touchstone Pictures/Album/Newscom, 21; Ron Sachs/picture-alliance/dpa/AP Images, 22; Bullstar/Shutterstock Images, 23; Warner Bros Digital Press Photos/Newscom, 25; Seth Wenig/AP Images, 26; Jeff T. Green/AP Images, 27

Library of Congress Cataloging-in-Publication Data
A catalog record for this book is available from the Library of Congress
978-1-63235-408-2 (hardcover)
978-1-63235-479-2 (paperback)
978-1-62143-531-0 (ebook)

Printed in the United States of America
022017

Access free, up-to-date content on this topic plus a full digital version of this book. Scan the QR code on page 31 or use your school's login at 12StoryLibrary.com.

Table of Contents

William Shakespeare Influences English Language 4

Mary Wollstonecraft Advances Women's Rights 6

Karl Marx and Friedrich Engels Promote Communism 8

Harriet Beecher Stowe Influences the Civil War 10

Charles Darwin Explains Evolution 12

George Orwell Predicts a Bleak Future 14

Langston Hughes Writes the Music of Harlem 16

Rachel Carson Inspires Environmentalists 18

Toni Morrison Shows Readers the Effects of Slavery 20

Amy Tan Shares the Immigrant Experience 22

J. K. Rowling Reignites Reading 24

Sherman Alexie Brings American Indians Out of the History Books 26

Other Notable Books 28

Glossary 30

For More Information 31

Index 32

About the Author 32

1
William Shakespeare Influences English Language

William Shakespeare was one of the greatest writers of all time. He is best known for his plays. They focus on timeless topics, such as love, jealousy, power, and death. Some of Shakespeare's most famous plays are *Hamlet*, *Romeo and Juliet*, and *Macbeth*. Actors sometimes performed his plays at the Globe Theatre in London, England.

During Shakespeare's lifetime, many of his plays were published individually. After Shakespeare's death, actors published

William Shakespeare lived from 1564 to 1616.

DID SHAKESPEARE DO ALL THE WRITING?

In the 1800s, scholars began to question William Shakespeare's works. They wondered if he really was the author of so many plays. Historians guessed that Sir Francis Bacon and even Queen Elizabeth I were among the true authors. How a single person could produce such an amazing body of work remains a mystery.

1,700

Approximate number of words William Shakespeare introduced into the English language.

- The first collection of Shakespeare's plays was published in 1623.
- Many everyday words and phrases come from his plays.
- Shakespeare's works are still performed and adapted for movies.

A reconstructed Globe Theatre in London, England, provides a place for actors to perform Shakespeare's plays.

a collection of his plays for the first time. The collection is called the First Folio, and it was printed in 1623. It included 36 of Shakespeare's 38 plays. If the First Folio had not been published, many of Shakespeare's plays might have been lost forever.

Publishing Shakespeare's works left a legacy in theater. It has allowed his plays to be staged for more than 400 years. Many actors consider performing a role in one of Shakespeare's plays to be proof of their skill. Filmmakers have also made the plays into movies. Some are loosely based on Shakespeare's plots. Others follow the original scripts closely.

Shakespeare's works also expanded the English language. He introduced English speakers to many new words and phrases. A few of those words include *bedazzle*, *gloomy*, and *grovel*. Phrases include *to thine own self be true*, which is from *Hamlet*, and *break the ice*, which comes from *The Taming of the Shrew*.

5

Mary Wollstonecraft Advances Women's Rights

In the 1700s, women had few rights. When a woman married, the property she owned was usually transferred to her husband. If a couple had children, the husband could make all the decisions about them, too. Most girls received little education beyond basic reading and math. Instead, they learned manners and skills to run a house.

An English writer named Mary Wollstonecraft wanted to change this. In 1792, she wrote *A Vindication of the Rights of Women*. In it, Wollstonecraft wrote that

6
Number of weeks it took Mary Wollstonecraft to write *A Vindication of the Rights of Women*.

- Mary Wollstonecraft wrote the one of the earliest books on the rights of women.
- She said every woman has the right to an education, a career, and a vote.
- Her book inspired women's rights activists throughout the twentieth century.

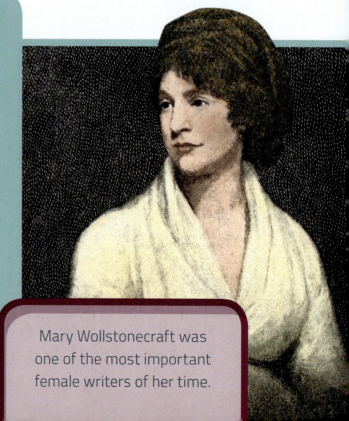

Mary Wollstonecraft was one of the most important female writers of her time.

Women across the world demanded more rights, including the right to vote.

women deserve the same respect and rights as men. She called for women's rights to education. Educated women, she argued, could help improve society. She suggested reforming England's entire education system to make this happen.

Wollstonecraft demanded other rights for women, too. She believed women should have the right to vote to help shape the nation's future. She also argued that if a woman wanted a career, she should be able to have one. Wollstonecraft believed society was missing out on skilled doctors, farmers, shopkeepers, and other professionals.

Wollstonecraft died in 1797, well before she could see her ideas put into practice. But her ideas lived on. In the early 1900s, her book inspired the fight for women's right to vote in the United States. Women turned to it again in the late 1960s and 1970s during the women's liberation movement.

Karl Marx and Friedrich Engels Promote Communism

Beginning in the 1750s, the way people lived in Europe started to change. People began to leave farms and move to cities. They took jobs in newly created factories. Life was hard for factory workers. They earned low wages and worked in dangerous conditions. In contrast, many factory owners grew rich.

Over time, these conditions made workers angry. This discontent led Germans Karl Marx and Friedrich Engels to write *The Communist Manifesto* in 1848. The pamphlet addressed problems in the working class. It talked about how lower-income people could end their struggles. It called for the workers of the world to unite through revolution. Then they could create a society without classes, in which all people were equal.

The Communist Manifesto was not very influential while Marx and Engels were alive. But it later became a guiding force for political change. In 1917, Vladimir Lenin led the world's first communist revolution. Other countries soon followed Lenin's lead.

2

Rank of *The Communist Manifesto* on a list of the best-selling books of all time.

- *The Communist Manifesto* had more influence after its authors died.
- It sparked political revolutions in two of the world's largest countries.
- It called for workers to end their struggles and unite.

Karl Marx's ideas have influenced millions of people for over a century.

In 1949, leader Mao Tse-tung led a communist revolution in China.

Mao and Lenin hoped to spread communism to other parts of the world. The United States and many countries in Europe feared this possibility. They wanted the world to be capitalist. In this system, citizens own a nation's businesses.

In contrast, in communism the government owns all of a nation's businesses. US forces fought wars in Korea and Vietnam to stop the spread of communism.

4

Harriet Beecher Stowe Influences the Civil War

In the 1850s, Americans increasingly began to speak out against slavery. One of the white people who became involved in this movement was Harriet Beecher Stowe. Stowe and her husband lived in Cincinnati, Ohio. Across from Cincinnati's Ohio River was the state of Kentucky, where slavery was legal.

During her 18 years living in Cincinnati, Stowe spoke with many enslaved people who had escaped. She learned about the hard

Harriet Beecher Stowe

THE BOOK THAT STARTED THE CIVIL WAR?

Harriet Beecher Stowe's book influenced the opinions of many people in the North. According to legend, when President Abraham Lincoln met author Harriet Beecher Stowe, he supposedly said, "So you're the little woman whose book started this Great War."

lives enslaved people endured. Stowe and her family moved to Maine in 1850. At that time, she decided to write a book about slavery. The result of her work was *Uncle Tom's Cabin*.

Stowe's story first appeared as a serial in the abolitionist newspaper *National Era* between 1851 and 1852. It was also published as a book in 1852. *Uncle Tom's Cabin* told the story of escaped slaves. It showed sides of slavery that people in the North had never seen before.

Stowe's book was an instant success. In its first year, it sold 300,000 copies. It was made into plays in many cities. The book and its message changed the way some people in the North viewed slavery. Many people believe it had such a large influence that it was one of the causes of the US Civil War (1861–1865).

10,000
Number of copies *Uncle Tom's Cabin* sold in its first week.

- Harriet Beecher Stowe met many escaped slaves while living in Cincinnati, Ohio.
- *Uncle Tom's Cabin* showed sides of slavery people in the North had never seen before.
- Many historians cite Stowe's book as a leading cause of the US Civil War.

The character Tom befriends a slaveholder's young daughter, Eva.

5

Charles Darwin Explains Evolution

In Europe in the 1800s, most people looked to the Bible to explain the world around them. The Bible describes how God created the world in seven days. Most Europeans at the time believed the world had not changed since God created it. They believed God had made each species separately. They also believed humans were made to rule all the species.

English scientist Charles Darwin questioned these ideas. Darwin was a scientist who was interested in living creatures. From 1831 to 1836, Darwin joined a crew aboard the HMS *Beagle*. The ship sailed to South America and circled the globe. Darwin served as the ship's naturalist.

Darwin studied finches on the Galapagos Islands near Ecuador.

THINK ABOUT IT

What kind of evidence would Darwin have needed to make his claims? What made Darwin's ideas controversial?

22

Age of Charles Darwin when he started out on his voyage aboard the HMS *Beagle*.

- Charles Darwin spent five years traveling the globe and studying animals.
- He wrote that animals can change over time to thrive in their environment.
- Darwin's ideas formed the base of modern biology.

While on the journey, Darwin observed animals from many different parts of the world. He found fossils of extinct animals. He began to believe that animals changed over time. They adapted to the conditions in which they lived. Only the fittest survived. Darwin also believed that all species had not been created separately. He believed they evolved from a common ancestor.

In 1859, Darwin published his ideas in a book called *On the Origin of Species*. It became the base of modern biology. For the next 150 years, scientists built on Darwin's ideas. His ideas helped doctors figure out how to fight diseases. They also led to the discovery of DNA and the study of how traits are passed down.

Charles Darwin's ideas caused controversy because they challenged religious beliefs.

George Orwell Predicts a Bleak Future

Beginning in the 1930s, the world had a series of all-powerful leaders. They controlled their countries with complete power. No one could question their authority. Adolf Hitler ruled this way in Germany. In the Soviet Union, it was Joseph Stalin. Francisco Franco ruled Spain. China had Mao Tse-tung.

Many people feared this type of government in which one person had total control. In 1949, English author George Orwell wrote a book that explored this idea. Orwell called it *Nineteen Eighty-Four*. In the book, Orwell describes life in the future under a government that has total control over its people. The only

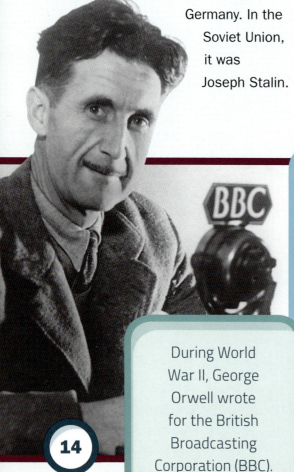

During World War II, George Orwell wrote for the British Broadcasting Corporation (BBC).

ORWELL'S ILLNESS

After World War II (1939–1945), Orwell moved to an island off Scotland. While there, Orwell was diagnosed with a lung disease called tuberculosis. At the time, he was in the middle of writing *Nineteen Eighty-Four*. Orwell admitted that his ill health affected his hopeless style of writing. He died in 1950, less than a year after *Nineteen Eighty-Four* was published.

300,000
Approximate number of copies of *Nineteen Eighty-Four* sold in the United States the first year after it was published.

- *Nineteen Eighty-Four* warned people about all-powerful governments.
- It told of a future where people lost rights to their thoughts, actions, and words.
- Orwell's warning is still relevant in the world today.

People refer to *Nineteen Eighty-Four* when they feel the government has overstepped its role.

person who is allowed to make decisions is the leader, who is called Big Brother.

Orwell's picture of the future is bleak. The government has cameras placed all over the country. They can observe people 24 hours a day. People can be punished for saying or doing anything against the government. Even having negative thoughts about the government is a crime. Citizens live in fear of Big Brother watching their every action and thought.

Nineteen Eighty-Four was a warning. Orwell wanted people to imagine how life would be if the government controlled every part of their lives, including private thoughts. After the book was published, Orwell's name took on a new meaning. "Orwellian" now describes anything that prevents a free and open society. The phrase "Big Brother is watching" now refers to any government that is monitoring its citizens too closely.

7

Langston Hughes Writes the Music of Harlem

Black people started moving to Harlem, New York, in the 1880s. It became known as the center of African American culture in New York City. The neighborhood was mostly black by the 1920s. As black people moved in, many white people moved out. But some white Harlem residents pushed back. Racial tensions were high during the 1920s and 1930s.

341,000
Estimated number of black people in Harlem in 1950.

- Harlem is a neighborhood in New York City.
- Art by black residents flourished in the 1920s and 1930s in a movement called the Harlem Renaissance.
- Langston Hughes was one of the most famous writers from the Harlem Renaissance.
- His work depicted the real struggles of black people and captured the spirit of Harlem.

Hughes's devotion to jazz influenced his writing.

At the same time, however, art flourished. The Harlem Renaissance was a cultural movement in which black residents expressed themselves as writers, photographers, and musicians. Langston Hughes was a part this movement. He was a novelist, a reporter, a poet, and more.

Hughes's work portrayed the real life of black people living in Harlem. His 1951 poem, "Montage of a Dream Deferred," went a step further. It captured the sound of life in Harlem. Jazz music was on the rise, and Hughes's poem was written with its rhythm. The verses stop and start. They use jazz slang and terms. The poem has the sound of improvisation jazz is known for. But there was more than just what the poem sounded like. It had a lot to say.

The poem shouted out both the promise and the pitfalls of Harlem. The "dream deferred" was the hope of residents for a better life. And that dream was being pushed off. It wasn't being realized. The poem asks one question. "What happens to a dream deferred?" It has since become one of the most famous lines in American poetry.

> Hughes's poetry helped inspire the civil rights movement and the 1963 March on Washington.

8 Rachel Carson Inspires Environmentalists

For many years, people knew that insects carried diseases that could harm people. Mosquitos could give people yellow fever or malaria. Lice could carry typhus. If the insects could be killed safely, it would save thousands of lives. In 1939, scientist Paul Hermann Müller discovered that a chemical called DDT could kill insects quickly and effectively.

In World War II, the Allies used DDT on a large scale. They dusted 1.3 million people with

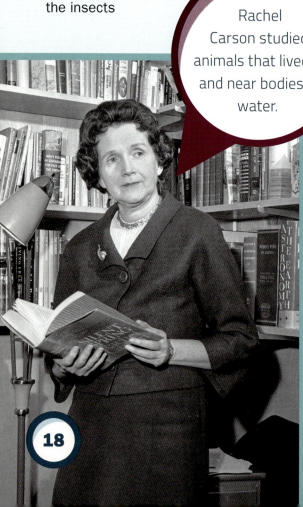

Rachel Carson studied animals that lived in and near bodies of water.

1972
Year the US government banned DDT except in emergency cases of a disease outbreak.

- DDT was widely used to kill insects that carried diseases.
- *Silent Spring* was the first book to address how people were hurting the environment.
- *Silent Spring* launched the environmental movement.

DDT to stop a typhus outbreak in Italy in 1944. Allies also sprayed DDT in Asia to kill mosquitos before troops arrived. DDT was so effective that after the war, its use continued. Cases of malaria, yellow fever, and typhus dropped dramatically throughout the world.

DDT had saved many lives. But scientists wondered how it affected the environment. Rachel Carson published a book about it in 1962. The book was called *Silent Spring*. In it, Carson explained how DDT hurt birds and fish. Carson also thought DDT could contaminate the world's food supply. Humans who ate that food could be at risk for cancer.

Silent Spring alarmed readers. Up until Carson's book was published, most people had not understood the harmful effects of human actions on the environment. *Silent Spring* spurred people to action. It started the environmental movement. People demanded the government create standards for clean air and water. They also began to recycle, carpool, and use clean energy to help the earth. Today, people continue this work to protect the environment.

> People still spray DDT in areas where diseases such as malaria and Zika are a high risk.

THINK ABOUT IT

How can a writer make a difference on big issues such as protecting the planet? What evidence can a book present that spurs people to action? What issues would you want to study and write about?

19

9 Toni Morrison Shows Readers the Effects of Slavery

The end of the US Civil War also meant slavery was finally illegal. Enslaved people were now free. But life was not easy. Freed slaves were poor. They struggled to find work. They still faced prejudice from many white people.

Toni Morrison revisits the Civil War in her 1987 book *Beloved*. The subject of her novel is Sethe, a woman who was enslaved on a Kentucky plantation. After the war, Sethe settles near Cincinnati. She lives with her daughter, Denver, and another person who was enslaved named Paul D. Meanwhile, Sethe tries to get her life together. But her

Toni Morrison was awarded the Presidential Medal of Freedom in 2012.

Oprah Winfrey (center) played the character of Sethe in the film *Beloved*.

house is haunted by a ghost. Sethe believes the ghost is the spirit of her daughter who died at age two. That daughter's name was Beloved.

The book switches between the past and present. It explains Sethe's life as a slave and what she went through. *Beloved* is not a simple ghost story. Through Sethe, Morrison wanted readers to feel the effect of slavery on a person. Freed people wrestled with what they experienced during slavery just to survive.

In 1988, Morrison won the Pulitzer Prize for *Beloved*. It is still taught in schools and considered one of the best American novels. It was adapted into a film in 1998.

4
Number of books Toni Morrison wrote before writing *Beloved*.

- *Beloved* is the story of a woman who had been enslaved and is now haunted by her daughter's death.
- The story is told partly in the past to illustrate the hard life that enslaved people faced.
- The novel won the Pulitzer Prize in 1988.

10 Amy Tan Shares the Immigrant Experience

In 1882, Congress passed laws banning Chinese immigrants from coming to the United States. These laws remained in place until 1943. Amy Tan's parents came to California from China in the late 1940s. She was born in the United States. Her family was a member of a group of friends they called the Joy Luck Club. They shared the immigrant experience together.

In the 1980s, Tan wrote a book called *The Joy Luck Club*. The members of the club are four

3.3 million
Number of Chinese Americans in the United States in 2010.

- Amy Tan was born in the United States after her parents emigrated from China in the 1940s.
- Her family was part of a social club with other Chinese Americans.
- This experience was the basis of her book *The Joy Luck Club*.
- The novel is a realistic depiction of the immigrant experience.

Amy Tan has written 11 books.

Mah-jongg is played with 144 tiles.

Chinese immigrant women. They meet to play mah-jongg, a Chinese tile matching game. When one of the members dies, her daughter June replaces her.

June was born in the United States. She feels she has little in common with these women who emigrated from China. The story shifts back and forth in time. It shows what life was like for the older women when they lived in China. It also shows how things have changed for the next generation, now living in the United States.

Through these stories, readers learn about the struggles many immigrants face adjusting to life in America. The book is beloved not only for its realistic portrayal of immigrants. It also honestly shows mother and daughter relationships.

Tan was a finalist for the National Book Award. She also served as coproducer and coscreenwriter on the book's 1993 film adaptation.

REAL TRAGEDY

Amy Tan's own childhood had its share of tragedy, much like the characters in her book. When she was 15, her father and brother died six months apart. Her mother believed there was a curse that would kill the rest of the family. So she took Tan and her younger brother to see the world while they still could. The family lived for a while in Switzerland.

11

J. K. Rowling Reignites Reading

In the early 1990s, publishers noticed a trend. Children's books were not selling well. Cable television, video games, personal computers, and VCRs all competed for the attention of young readers. Everything changed in 1997. That year, J. K. Rowling's first book arrived in United Kingdom bookstores. Rowling's *Harry Potter and the Philosopher's Stone* introduced readers to an orphaned wizard named Harry Potter.

J. K. Rowling wrote the first Harry Potter book in coffee shops.

FROM JOANNE TO J. K.

When preparing to print the first Harry Potter book, the publishers worried that boys would not read a book written by a woman. They believed this might hurt sales. So they asked Rowling not to use her first name, which is Joanne. Instead, she used her initials: J. K. That way, readers would not know if Harry Potter's author was a man or a woman.

6

Number of years it took J. K. Rowling to write the first Harry Potter book.

- The Harry Potter books interested children in reading again.
- The first Harry Potter book won the British Book Award in 1997.
- Harry Potter's popularity spread across the world.

At first, Rowling's publishers only printed 500 copies of the book. They figured its sales would be as slow as other children's books. Then *Harry Potter and the Philosopher's Stone* won the British Book Award in 1997. The win created strong interest in the book. American publishers wanted to sell it in the United States. They changed the title to *Harry Potter and the Sorcerer's Stone*. In December 1998, the book first appeared on the *New York Times* Bestseller list. It stayed there for 79 weeks.

The movie version of *Harry Potter and the Sorcerer's Stone* was the highest-earning film in 2001.

Rowling continued writing about Harry Potter. In total, she created a series of seven books. Children grew excited to read them. The popularity of the series spread to other countries. Today, nearly 450 million copies of the books are in print. They have been translated into 73 languages. Rowling's best-selling series ignited a new desire to read among children and adults alike.

12 Sherman Alexie Brings American Indians Out of the History Books

Teenagers of America are used to reading about American Indians. They hear about them when studying about colonialism and the American Revolution. They hear the names of different American Indian nations and leaders such as Geronimo and Crazy Horse.

American Indians are often talked about as if they are people of the past. But they remain a part of American culture today. And they have stories to tell. Sherman Alexie certainly had one. He grew up on the Spokane Reservation in eastern Washington State. He witnessed the struggles of Spokane Indians living there. There was poverty, alcohol

Sherman Alexie (second from right) won the National Book Award for *The Absolutely True Diary of a Part-Time Indian.*

abuse, and hopelessness.

Alexie told his own story through the eyes of Arnold "Junior" Spirit Jr. in *The Absolutely True Diary of a Part-Time Indian*. The 2007 book was based on Alexie's life. It tells the story of Junior's first year of high school. To escape the trouble of the reservation, Junior changes schools. At his new high school, he is the only American Indian.

Junior deals with bullying. His friends back home are mad at him for leaving. But he finds a place to belong on the school basketball team. And he starts to adjust to his new world.

The book drew some criticism for its adult themes. It was even banned in some places. But Alexie was trying to depict life on the reservation as it really was. These were real challenges faced by real people. *The Absolutely True Diary of a Part-Time Indian* was more than just a novel. It showed readers that the story of American Indian nations did not end after they were forced onto reservations.

> Conflicts about how land in the Spokane Reservation can be used are ongoing.

156,000
Size, in acres (63,131 ha), of the Spokane Reservation.

- *The Absolutely True Diary of a Part-Time Indian* is about a high school Spokane Indian freshman named Junior.
- Sherman Alexie based the book on his own life.
- The book is controversial but realistically depicts the life of many modern-day American Indians.

Other Notable Books

Grimm's Fairy Tales by the Brothers Grimm

German librarians Jacob and Wilhelm Grimm collected fairy tales in the early 1800s. They published seven editions, and with each one, they made the stories more suitable for children. The brothers are credited with saving the fairy tale.

One Thousand and One Nights

A fictional king plans to execute his wife in the morning. To buy time, the queen begins telling a story every night so that the king will have to keep her alive to hear the ending. The hundreds of Middle Eastern and South Asian folktales she tells include memorable characters and mythologies that have captured the West's imagination since 1704.

One Hundred Years of Solitude by Gabriel García Márquez

One of the most influential Latin American texts of all time, this 1967 novel tells the story of seven generations of the Buendía family. The book introduced magical realism to readers worldwide and has sold more than 30 million copies. Gabriel García Márquez never agreed to sell the rights, so no movie adaptation has ever been made.

The Little Prince by Antoine de Saint-Exupéry

In this small book, an aviator narrates the story of a young prince who has come from his home on an asteroid. The book has been translated into more than 250 languages.

Glossary

contaminate
To make something impure by adding a poisonous substance.

liberation
The act of securing physical freedom or freedom of rights.

naturalist
A person who studies nature and its history.

pamphlet
A short booklet about one topic.

serial
A piece of writing that appears in installments in a magazine or journal.

translate
To change words from one language to another.

trend
A general direction in which something is headed.

For More Information

Books

Fabiny, Sarah. *Who Was Rachel Carson?* New York: Grosset & Dunlap, 2014.

Krull, Kathleen. *Charles Darwin.* New York: Viking, 2010.

Sutcliffe, Jane. *Will's Words: How William Shakespeare Changed the Way You Talk.* Watertown, MA: Charlesbridge, 2016.

Visit 12StoryLibrary.com

Scan the code or use your school's login at **12StoryLibrary.com** for recent updates about this topic and a full digital version of this book. Enjoy free access to:

- Digital ebook
- Breaking news updates
- Live content feeds
- Videos, interactive maps, and graphics
- Additional web resources

Note to educators: Visit 12StoryLibrary.com/register to sign up for free premium website access. Enjoy live content plus a full digital version of every 12-Story Library book you own for every student at your school.

Editor's note: The 12 topics featured in this book are selected by the author and approved by the book's editor. While not a definitive list, the selected topics are an attempt to balance the book's subject with the intended readership. To expand learning about this subject, please visit **12StoryLibrary.com** or use this book's QR code to access free additional content.

Index

Absolutely True Diary of a Part-Time Indian, The, 26–27
Alexie, Sherman, 26–27

Beloved, 20–21

Carson, Rachel, 18–19
Communist Manifesto, The, 8–9

Darwin, Charles, 12–13

Engels, Friedrich, 8–9

Hamlet, 4, 5
Harlem Renaissance, 16–17
Harry Potter and the Philosopher's Stone, 24–25
Hughes, Langston, 16–17

Joy Luck Club, The, 22–23

Macbeth, 4
Marx, Karl, 8–9
"Montage of a Dream Deferred," 17
Morrison, Toni, 20–21

Nineteen Eighty-Four, 14–15

On the Origin of the Species, 13
Orwell, George, 14–15

Romeo and Juliet, 4
Rowling, J. K., 24–25

Shakespeare, William, 4–5
Silent Spring, 18–19
Stowe, Harriet Beecher, 10–11

Taming of the Shrew, The, 5
Tan, Amy, 22–23

Uncle Tom's Cabin, 10–11

Vindication of the Rights of Women, A, 6–7

Wollstonecraft, Mary, 6–7

About the Author

Barbara Krasner has been an avid reader ever since she can remember. She teaches *The Adventures of Alice in Wonderland*, *Little Women*, and *Treasure Island* to children's literature classes at universities in New Jersey. She is the author of more than 20 books for young readers.

READ MORE FROM 12-STORY LIBRARY

Every 12-Story Library book is available in many formats. For more information, visit 12StoryLibrary.com.